"Soren Lorensen would like to
drink his pink milk all by himself,
with just me on his own."

"Now," says Lola.

"It was fun to **play** with you and Marv, but please DON'T do bothering or **interrupting**..."

"See!" shouts Lola,
"I **told** you Soren Lorensen knew how to
catch the most strangest and
TRICKY creature."

"How did he do it?" I say.

"Well," says Lola,
"EVERYBODY loves tea parties."

"So who gets to drink the
pink milk?" says Marv.

"Oh, that is for
Soren Lorensen,"
says Lola.

"Catching strange
and tricky creatures
makes him quite
thirsty."

And there is
no escape for
the MOST STRANGE
and
terrifyingly **tricky** creature
in the
universe.

And just like that

we have

CAUGHT
HIM.

AND THEN THERE HE IS,

the most **strange** and terrifyingly **tricky**
creature in the universe
about to gobble us up . . .

"Show him
the rabbit!"

says Lola.

Lola says,
"If there are
no such things as
invisible voices,
then
why can't
you hear him?"

"SSSH," I whisper.
"Something is
coming."

"I can't hear him talking," says Marv.

"You can't **hear** him because he is INVISIBLE," says Lola.

"You CAN hear invisible people," I say.

Lola says, "Not Soren Lorensen because his **voice** is invisible **too.**"

Marv says, "There are no such things as **invisible** voices."

And Lola whispers,
"Sssh, Soren Lorensen is
talking and he says we
must be very,

extremely
quiet.

Don't
make
even a
squeak."

Soon we find ourselves
right in the middle of the
deep, dark forest where
the MOST STRANGE and
terrifyingly **tricky**
creature lives.

frightened of rabbits." I say, "But why do we need a little cart?"

Lola says, "For the pink milk of course."

are creatures Tricky up. you gobbling creature the stop "To And Lola says,

Mary says, "What is the pink milk for, Lola?"

And Lola says, "You will see."

So we all set off to find the
MOST STRANGE and terrifyingly tricky
creature in the universe.

I say, "What is the tea set for, Lola?"

And she says, "Tricky creatures love tea."

And Marv says,

"What is the rabbit for, Lola?"

"Oh yes," says Lola.
"All you will need is
a tea set
and a little cart
and also a rabbit of course."

"REALLY?" I say.

"Oh yes,
and you MUST
absolutely get one or
three glasses of
pink milk too."

"WHAT?
all of the
pink milk?"
says Marv.

"Yes,
completely,"
says Lola.

"Lola," I say, "now we will never catch the MOST STRANGE and terrifyingly **tricky** creature in the universe."

"Why not?" says Lola.

"Because we can't CREEP UP on him," says Marv.

"Don't worry," says Lola, "Soren Lorensen will **catch** him."

"Really?" I say.

"That's because there is
NO such person as
Soren Lorensen," I say.

"Well, if there is
no such
person,

"My friend, Soren Lorensen,"
                              says Lola.

I say, "LOLA, did you drink our
                              invisibility potion?"
Lola says,
"Oh, I only had a small sip.
Soren Lorensen had much more than
                              I did, that's why he is more
                              invisible than me."

I say, "You are NOT INVISIBLE,
not even one bit."

"How do you know?" says Lola.

"Because we can SEE you
of course," says Marv.

And Lola says,
"You can only see me because
you know what I look like.
You can't see Soren Lorensen
                              at all."

"Who are you talking to?" I say.

"I am over here, you probably cannot see me because I am invisible."

But
when I
look under
Mum and Dad's
bed there she is,
talking
away.

"Lola!" I shout, "What have you done with our potion?"
But Lola is nowhere to be seen.
We look **everywhere**.

But all we can hear is a tiny voice . . .

It sounds like it is coming from a long way away.

"where are you?"

I shout.

But when we go into the kitchen,
we get a bit of a fright
because there
is the
STRANGE and
terrifyingly **tricky**
creature
looking very hungry
indeed.

There is
no escape.

but not **one** single **tricky** one,

we decide to

have a **snack**.

Sailing around
the world can
make you quite
peckish.

We leave it in the fridge and
when we have sailed
twice around the world
and seen some
EXTREMELY
strange
creatures

So Marv and me invent an **invisibility** potion.

It is made from pink milk, a tiny drop of banana

and a **secret INVISIBLE INGREDIENT** that no one can see except us.

"LOLA!" I say,
"Will you STOP bothering us
and interrupting!"

Lola says,
"I will NOT
do
bothering and I will
NOT do interrupting.
You won't even
know
I am here."

"What's it **top secret** for?" says Lola.

"It's a potion for helping us catch **strange** and **tricky** creatures," says Marv.

"Oh," says Lola. "How does it **do that**?"

"By turning you **invisible**," Marv says.

"Oh," says Lola.

"Would you maybe like to have a **tea party** instead?"

So this time I said,

"Today Lola, just for once,
I want to play with Marv
by **myself** on
my own.

You see we are inventing a
very **inventive** invention."

"What **is** it?" says Lola.

"It's **top secret**," I say.

terrifyingly tricky creature in the UNIVERSE,

Lola's rabbit made a squeaking noise and he ran off.

And yesterday,

just when

Marv and me   were

creeping up   on   the   most STRANGE   and

Lola said she wanted to take it for a ride in her cart.

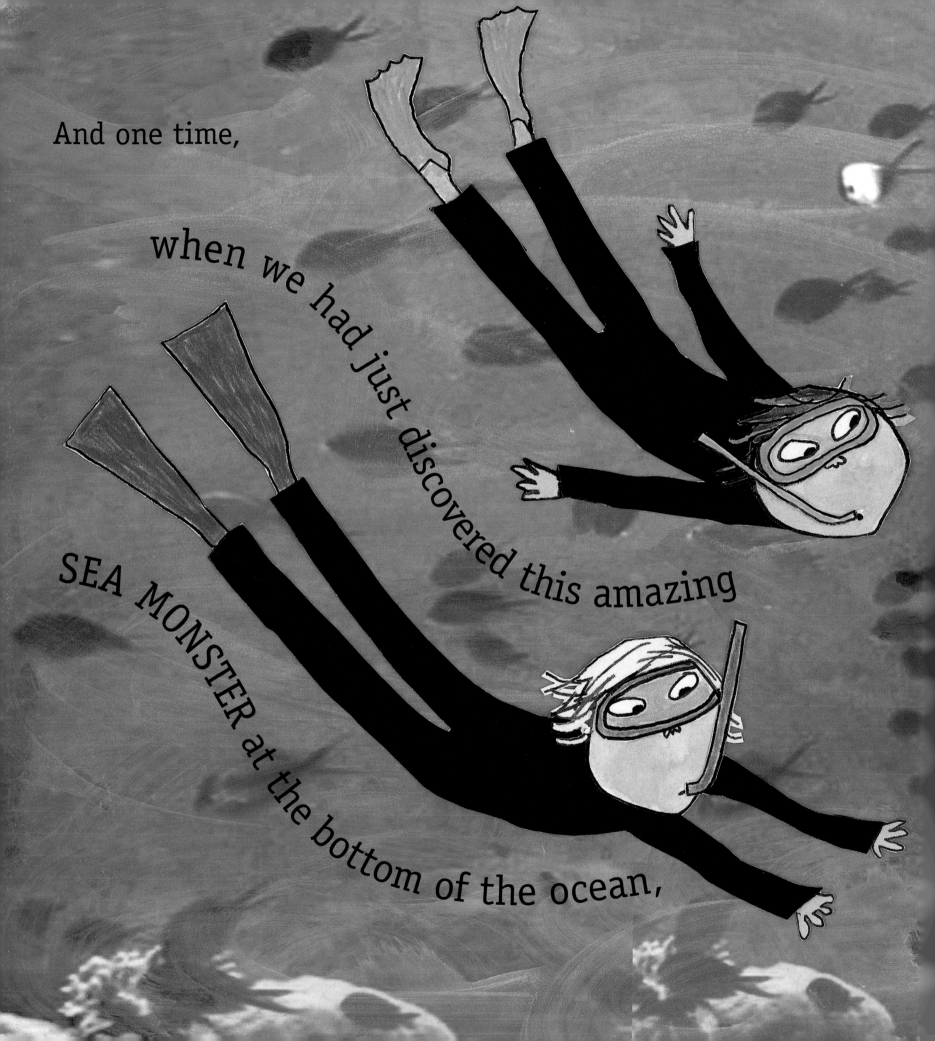

And one time,

when we had just discovered this amazing

SEA MONSTER at the bottom of the ocean,

and Lola stepped on our spaceship.

We had to **walk** back to Earth.

Lola does
not think
this is fun.

Most of the time this is fine.
But sometimes I just want to be by myself
ON MY OWN with just Marv.

Marv is my best friend and usually we like
to spend our time looking for strange
and **tricky** creatures.

I have this little sister Lola.
She is small and very funny.
She always wants to know what I am up to and
she always wants to do what I am doing.
She NEVER wants to be anywhere without me.